For Mum and Dad, thank you for everything (xox) —S.P.

For Nia, a massive thanks for all your help! —K.H.

STERLING CHILDREN'S BOOKS
New York

An Imprint of Sterling Publishing Co., Inc.
1166 Avenue of the Americas
New York, NY 10036

Text © 2016 by Simon Philip

Illustrations © 2016 by Kate Hindley

First Sterling edition published in 2017.
Published by arrangement with Simon & Schuster UK Ltd.

ISBN 978-1-4549-2688-7

Distributed in Canada by Sterling Publishing
c/o Canadian Manda Group, 664 Annette Street
Toronto, Ontario, Canada M6S 2C8

For information about custom editions, special sales, and premium and corporate purchases, please contact Sterling Special Sales at 800-805-5489 or specialsales@sterlingpublishing.com.

Manufactured in China

Lot #:
2 4 6 8 10 9 7 5 3
11/17

www.sterlingpublishing.com

YOU MUST BRING A HAT!

Simon Philip
& Kate Hindley

STERLING CHILDREN'S BOOKS
New York

I received an invitation to a party.

Immediately I panicked.
I DIDN'T OWN A HAT!

And the invitation specifically
stated that I MUST bring a hat.

The party depended on it.

I searched everywhere for a hat.

Since he wouldn't negotiate,
I was left with no choice.

At least I had a hat. Even if it
was still attached to a monkey.

But on arrival, the security was pretty tight.

"Invitation, please," said the doorman.
Apparently there were other rules, too.
**"Sorry, sir, but we're under strict instructions
not to let in any hat-wearing monkeys . . .**

unless they are also
wearing a monocle."

Luckily, we soon bumped into a badger named Geoff.
He was just the sort of badger we required.

*"I do beg your pardon, chaps,
but are you, by any chance,
after a monocle?"*

"Indeed we are.
We need it for a party."

"I will lend this monkey my monocle on the condition . . .

that I may accompany you to your shindig."

"Invitation, please,"
the doorman said again.

**"Sorry, sir, but we're under strict instructions
not to let in any hat-and-monocle-wearing monkeys
if they are accompanied by a badger named Geoff . . .**

**unless Geoff
can play the piano."**

"Can you play the piano?" I asked.

"Don't insult me.
I'm a badger!
Of course I can."

"Geoff can play," I said firmly.

"I'm afraid we need to see that," the doorman replied.

Geoff was GREAT on the piano.
But we still had a problem.

**"Sorry, sir, but we can't let this piano-lending elephant in.
He's not wearing a tutu."**

Just my luck! There's NEVER a tutu around when you need one.

We solved that problem surprisingly quickly.
Surely NOW we'd be allowed in?

But we'd failed to notice the sign.

Ah.

Martin kindly helped us out. And, as he was a very clever penguin, we were already prepared for the next rule:

"All penguins accompanying pink-tutu-wearing elephants MUST bring with them a suitcase full of cheese."

But it turned out the cheese needed to be sliced,
and none of us had thought to bring a knife.

And that was when I'd had ENOUGH!

"LOOK, THESE ARE THE SILLIEST RULES I'VE EVER HEARD. NIGEL CLEARLY INVITATION THAT I COULD BRING SO LONG AS I BROUGHT A HAT, A MONKEY IN A HAT SO I BROUGHT A HAT

"Nigel?"
said the doorman.
"Who's Nigel?
This is Felicity's party."

"This isn't number 32?"

"Next door."

Oops.

Still, Nigel's party was worth the hassle . . .

Even if we WERE a little late.